In Our Time and Other Stories

BESTSELLING FICTION

- 1984 by George Orwell
  Fiction/Classics, ISBN: 9788193545836

- Animal Farm by George Orwell
  Fiction/Classics, ISBN: 9789387669062

- Anthem by Ayn Rand
  Fiction/Classics, ISBN: 9789389157178

- As a Man Thinketh by James Allen
  Fiction/Classics, ISBN: 9789388118422

- Demian by Hermann Hesse
  Fiction/Classics, ISBN: 9789388118170

- Gitanjali by Rabindranath Tagore
  Fiction/Poems, ISBN: 9789387669079

- Mansarover 1 (Hindi) by Premchand
  Fiction/Short Stories, ISBN: 9789387669086

- Selected Stories of Rabindranath Tagore by Tagore
  Fiction/Short Stories, ISBN: 9789387669307

- Siddhartha by Hermann Hesse
  Fiction/Classics, ISBN: 9789387669116

- Tales from India by Rudyard Kipling
  Fiction/Short Stories, ISBN: 9789387669123

- Tales from Shakespeare by Charles Lamb, Mary Lamb
  Fiction/Short Stories, ISBN: 9789387669314

- The Jungle Book by Rudyard Kipling
  Children's/Classics, ISBN: 9789387669338

- The Light of Asia by Sir Edwin Arnold
  Fiction/Poetry, ISBN: 9789387669130

- The Prophet by Kahlil Gibran
  Fiction/Classics, ISBN: 9789388118453

Search the book by its ISBN

IN OUR TIME

AND OTHER STORIES

Ernest Hemingway

GENERAL PRESS

Published by

GENERAL PRESS

4805/24, Fourth Floor, Krishna House
Ansari Road, Daryaganj, New Delhi - 110002
Ph : 011-23282971, 45795759
E-mail : generalpressindia@gmail.com

www.generalpress.in

First Edition : 2022

ISBN : 9789354991608

Published by Azeem Ahmad Khan for General Press

Contents

IN OUR TIME

1

Everybody was drunk. The whole battery was drunk going along the road in the dark. We were going to the Champagne. The lieutenant kept riding his horse out into the fields and saying to him, "I'm drunk, I tell you, mon vieux. Oh, I am so soused." We went along the road all night in the dark and the adjutant kept riding up alongside my kitchen and saying, "You must put it out. It is dangerous. It will be observed." We were fifty kilometers from the front but the adjutant worried about the fire in my kitchen. It was funny going along that road. That was when I was a kitchen corporal.

2

The first matador got the horn through his sword hand and the crowd hooted him out. The second matador slipped and the bull caught him through the belly and he hung on to the horn with one hand and held the other tight against the place, and the bull rammed him wham against the wall and the horn came out, and he lay in the sand, and then got up like crazy drunk and tried to slug the men carrying him away and yelled for his sword but he fainted. The kid came out and had to kill five bulls because you can't have more than three matadors, and the last bull he was so tired he couldn't get the sword in. He couldn't hardly lift his arm. He tried five times and the crowd was quiet because it was a good bull and it looked like him or the bull and then he finally made it. He sat down in the sand and puked and they held a cape over him while the crowd hollered and threw things down into the bull ring.

3

Minarets stuck up in the rain out of Adrianople across the mud flats. The carts were jammed for thirty miles along the Karagatch road. Water buffalo and cattle were hauling carts through the mud. No end and no beginning. Just carts loaded with everything they owned. The old men and women, soaked through, walked along keeping the cattle moving. The Maritza was running yellow almost up to the bridge. Carts were jammed solid on the bridge with camels bobbing along through them. Greek cavalry herded along the procession. Women and kids were in the carts crouched with mattresses, mirrors, sewing machines, bundles. There was a woman having a kid with a young girl holding a blanket over her and crying. Scared sick looking at it. It rained all through the evacuation.

4

We were in a garden at Mons. Young Buckley came in with his patrol from across the river. The first German I saw climbed up over the garden wall. We waited till he got one leg over and then potted him. He had so much equipment on and looked awfully surprised and fell down into the garden. Then three more came over further down the wall. We shot them. They all came just like that.

5

It was a frightfully hot day. We'd jammed an absolutely perfect barricade across the bridge. It was simply priceless. A big old wrought iron grating from the front of a house. Too heavy to lift and you could shoot through it and they would have to climb over it. It was absolutely topping. They tried to get over it, and we potted them from forty yards. They rushed it, and officers came out alone and worked on it. It was an absolutely perfect obstacle.

Their officers were very fine. We were frightfully put out when we heard the flank had gone, and we had to fall back.

6

They shot the six cabinet ministers at half-past six in the morning against the wall of a hospital. There were pools of water in the courtyard. There were wet dead leaves on the paving of the courtyard. It rained hard. All the shutters of the hospital were nailed shut. One of the ministers was sick with typhoid. Two soldiers carried him downstairs and out into the rain. They tried to hold him up against the wall but he sat down in a puddle of water. The other five stood very quietly against the wall. Finally the officer told the soldiers it was no good trying to make him stand up. When they fired the first volley he was sitting down in the water with his head on his knees.

7

Nick sat against the wall of the church where they had dragged him to be clear of machine gun fire in the street. Both legs stuck out awkwardly. He had been hit in the spine. His face was sweaty and dirty. The sun shone on his face.

The day was very hot. Rinaldi, big backed, his equipment sprawling, lay face downward against the wall. Nick looked straight ahead brilliantly. The pink wall of the house opposite had fallen out from the roof, and an iron bedstead hung twisted toward the street. Two Austrian dead lay in the rubble in the shade of the house. Up the street were other dead. Things were getting forward in the town. It was going well. Stretcher bearers would be along any time now. Nick turned his head carefully and looked down at Rinaldi. "Senta Rinaldi. Senta. You and me we've made a separate peace." Rinaldi lay still in the sun breathing with difficulty. "Not patriots." Nick turned his head carefully away smiling sweatily. Rinaldi was a disappointing audience.

8

While the bombardment was knocking the trench to pieces at Fossalta, he lay very flat and sweated and prayed oh jesus christ get me out of here. Dear jesus please get me out. Christ please please please christ. If you'll only keep me from getting killed I'll do anything you say. I believe in you and I'll tell everyone in the world that you are the only thing that matters. Please please dear jesus. The shelling moved further up the line. We went to work on the trench and in the morning the sun came up and the day was hot and muggy and cheerful and quiet. The next night back at Mestre he did not tell the girl he went upstairs with at the Villa Rossa about Jesus. And he never told anybody.

9

At two o'clock in the morning two Hungarians got into a cigar store at Fifteenth Street and Grand Avenue. Drevitts and Boyle drove up from the Fifteenth Street police station in a Ford. The Hungarians were backing their wagon out of an alley. Boyle shot one off the seat of the wagon and one out of the wagon box. Drevetts got frightened when he found they were both dead. Hell Jimmy, he said, you oughtn't to have done it. There's liable to be a hell of a lot of trouble.

—They're crooks ain't they? said Boyle. They're wops ain't they? Who the hell is going to make any trouble?

—That's all right maybe this time, said Drevitts, but how did you know they were wops when you bumped them?

Wops, said Boyle, I can tell wops a mile off.

10

One hot evening in Milan they carried him up onto the roof and he could look out over the top of the town. There were chimney swifts in the sky. After a while it got dark and the searchlights came out. The others went down and took the bottles with them. He and Ag could hear them below on the balcony. Ag sat on the bed. She was cool and fresh in the hot night.

Ag stayed on night duty for three months. They were glad to let her. When they operated on him she prepared him for the operating table, and they had a joke about friend or enema. He went under the anæsthetic holding tight on to himself so that he would not blab about anything during the silly, talky time. After he got on crutches he used to take the temperature so Ag would not have to get up from the bed. There were only a few patients, and they all knew about it. They all liked Ag. As he walked back along the halls he thought of Ag in his bed.

Before he went back to the front they went into the Duomo and prayed. It was dim and quiet, and there were other people praying. They wanted to get married, but there was not enough time for the banns, and neither of them had birth certificates. They felt as though they were married, but they wanted everyone to knew about it, and to make it so they could not lose it.

Ag wrote him many letters that he never got until after the armistice. Fifteen came in a bunch and he sorted them by the dates and read them all straight through. They were about the hospital, and how much she loved him and how it was impossible to get along without him and how terrible it was missing him at night.

After the armistice they agreed he should go home to get a job so they might be married. Ag would not come home until he had a good job and could come to New York to meet her. It was understood he would not drink, and he did not want to see his friends or anyone in the States. Only to get a job and be married. On the train from Padova to Milan they quarrelled about her not being willing to come home at once. When they had to say good-bye in the station at Padova they kissed good-bye, but were not finished with the quarrel. He felt sick about saying good-bye like that.

He went to America on a boat from Genoa. Ag went back to Torre di Mosta to open a hospital. It was lonely and rainy there, and there was a battalion of *arditi* quartered in the town. Living in the muddy, rainy town in the winter the major of the battalion made love to Ag, and she had never known Italians before, and finally wrote a letter to the States that theirs had been only a boy and girl affair. She was sorry, and she knew he would probably not be able to understand, but might someday forgive her, and be grateful to her, and she expected, absolutely unexpectedly, to be married in the spring. She loved him as always, but she realized now it was only a boy and girl love. She hoped he would have a great career, and believed in him absolutely. She knew it was for the best.

The Major did not marry her in the spring, or any other time. Ag never got an answer to her letter to Chicago about it. A short time after he contracted gonorrhea from a sales girl from The Fair riding in a taxicab through Lincoln Park.

11

In 1919 he was travelling on the railroads in Italy carrying a square of oilcloth from the headquarters of the party written in indelible pencil and saying here was a comrade who had suffered very much under the whites in Budapest and requesting comrades to aid him in any way. He used this instead of a ticket. He was very shy and quite young and the train men passed him on from one crew to another. He had no money, and they fed him behind the counter in railway eating houses.

He was delighted with Italy. It was a beautiful country he said. The people were all kind. He had been in many towns, walked much and seen many pictures. Giotto, Masaccio, and Piero della Francesca he bought reproductions of and carried them wrapped in a copy of *Avanti*. Mantegna he did not like.

He reported at Bologna, and I took him with me up into the Romagna where it was necessary I go to see a man. We had a good trip together. It was early September and the country was pleasant. He was a Magyar, a very nice boy and very shy. Horthy's men had done some bad things to him. He talked about it a little. In spite of Italy, he believed altogether in the world revolution.

—But how is the movement going in Italy? he asked.

—Very badly, I said.

—But it will go better, he said. You have everything here. It is the one country that everyone is sure of. It will be the starting point of everything.

At Bologna he said good-bye to us to go on the train to Milano and then to Aosta to walk over the pass into Switzerland. I spoke to him about the Mantegnas in Milano. No, he said, very shyly, he did not like Mantegna. I wrote out for him where to eat in Milano and the addresses of comrades. He thanked me very much, but his mind was already looking forward to walking over the pass. He was very eager to walk over the pass while the weather held good. The last I heard of him the Swiss had him in jail near Sion.

12

They whack whacked the white horse on the legs and he knee-ed himself up. The picador twisted the stirrups straight and pulled and hauled up into the saddle. The horse's entrails hung down in a blue bunch and swung backward and forward as he began to canter, the *monos* whacking him on the back of his legs with the rods. He cantered jerkily along the barrera. He stopped stiff and one of the *monos* held his bridle and walked him forward. The picador kicked in his spurs, leaned forward and shook his lance at the bull. Blood pumped regularly from between the horse's front legs. He was nervously wobbly. The bull could not make up his mind to charge.

13

The crowd shouted all the time and threw pieces of bread down into the ring, then cushions and leather wine bottles, keeping up whistling and yelling. Finally the bull was too tired from so much bad sticking and folded his knees and lay down and one of the *cuadrilla* leaned out over his neck and killed him with the *puntillo*. The crowd came over the barrera and around the torero and two men grabbed him and held him and someone cut off his pigtail and was waving it and a kid grabbed it and ran away with it. Afterwards I saw him at the café. He was very short with a brown face and quite drunk and he said after all it has happened before like that. I am not really a good bull fighter.

14

If it happened right down close in front of you, you could see Villalta snarl at the bull and curse him, and when the bull charged he swung back firmly like an oak when the wind hits it, his legs tight together, the muleta trailing and the sword following the curve behind. Then he cursed the bull, flopped the muleta at him, and swung back from the charge his feet firm, the muleta curving and each swing the crowd roaring.

When he started to kill it was all in the same rush. The bull looking at him straight in front, hating. He drew out the sword from the folds of the muleta and sighted with the same movement and called to the bull, Toro! Toro! and the bull charged and Villalta charged and just for a moment they became one. Villalta became one with the bull and then it was over. Villalta standing straight and the red kilt of the sword sticking out dully between the bull's shoulders. Villalta, his hand up at the crowd and the bull roaring blood, looking straight at Villalta and his legs caving.

15

I heard the drums coming down the street and then the fifes and the pipes and then they came around the corner, all dancing. The street full of them. Maera saw him and then I saw him. When they stopped the music for the crouch he hunched down in the street with them all and when they started it again he jumped up and went dancing down the street with them. He was drunk all right.

You go down after him, said Maera, he hates me.

So I went down and caught up with them and grabbed him while he was crouched down waiting for the music to break loose and said, Come on Luis. For Christ sake you've got bulls this afternoon. He didn't listen to me, he was listening so hard for the music to start.

I said, Don't be a damn fool Luis. Come on back to the hotel.

Then the music started up again and he jumped up and twisted away from me and started dancing. I grabbed his arm and he pulled loose and said, Oh leave me alone. You're not my father.

I went back to the hotel and Maera was on the balcony looking out to see if I'd be bringing him back. He went inside when he saw me and came downstairs disgusted.

Well, I said, after all he's just an ignorant Mexican savage.

Yes, Maera said, and who will kill his bulls after he gets a *cogida?*

We, I suppose, I said.

Yes, we, said Maera. We kills the savages' bulls, and the drunkards' bulls, and the *riau-riau* dancers' bulls. Yes. We kill them. We kill them all right. Yes. Yes. Yes.

16

Maera lay still, his head on his arms, his face in the sand. He felt warm and sticky from the bleeding. Each time he felt the horn coming. Sometimes the bull only bumped him with his head. Once the horn went all the way through him and he felt it go into the sand. Someone had the bull by the tail. They were swearing at him and flopping the cape in his face. Then the bull was gone. Some men picked Maera up and started to run with him toward the barriers through the gate out the passage way around under the grand stand to the infirmary. They laid Maera down on a cot and one of the men went out for the doctor. The others stood around. The doctor came running from the corral where he had been sewing up picador horses. He had to stop and wash his hands. There was a great shouting going on in the grandstand overhead. Maera wanted to say something and found he could not talk. Maera felt everything getting larger and larger and then smaller and smaller. Then it got larger and larger and larger and then smaller and smaller. Then everything commenced to run faster and faster as when they speed up a cinematograph film. Then he was dead.

17

They hanged Sam Cardinella at six o'clock in the morning in the corridor of the county jail. The corridor was high and narrow with tiers of cells on either side. All the cells were occupied. The men had been brought in for the hanging. Five men sentenced to be hanged were in the five top cells. Three of the men to be hanged were negroes. They were very frightened. One of the white men sat on his cot with his head in his hands. The other lay flat on his cot with a blanket wrapped around his head.

They came out onto the gallows through a door in the wall. There were six or seven of them including two priests. They were carrying Sam Cardinella. He had been like that since about four o'clock in the morning.

While they were strapping his legs together two guards held him up and the two priests were whispering to him. "Be a man, my son," said one priest. When they came toward him with the cap to go over his head Sam Cardinella lost control of his sphincter muscle. The guards who had been holding him up dropped him. They were both disgusted. "How about a chair, Will?" asked one of the guards, "Better get one," said a man in a derby hat.

When they all stepped back on the scaffolding back of the drop, which was very heavy, built of oak and steel and swung on ball bearings, Sam Cardinella was left sitting there strapped tight, the younger of the two priests kneeling beside the chair. The priest skipped back onto the scaffolding just before the drop fell.

18

The king was working in the garden. He seemed very glad to see me. We walked through the garden. This is the queen, he said. She was clipping a rose bush. Oh how do you do, she said. We sat down at a table under a big tree and the king ordered whiskey and soda. We have good whiskey anyway, he said. The revolutionary committee, he told me, would not allow him to go outside the palace grounds. Plastiras is a very good man I believe, he said, but frightfully difficult. I think he did right though shooting those chaps. If Kerensky had shot a few men things might have been altogether different. Of course the great thing in this sort of an affair is not to be shot oneself!

It was very jolly. We talked for a long time. Like all Greeks he wanted to go to America.

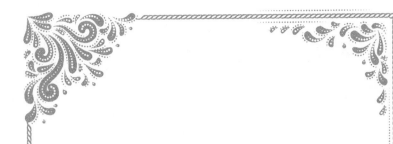

A CLEAN WELL LIGHTED PLACE

It was late and every one had left the cafe except an old man who sat in the shadow the leaves of the tree made against the electric light. In the day time the street was dusty; but at night the dew settled the dust and the old man liked to sit late because he was deaf and now at night it was quiet and he felt the difference. The two waiters inside the cafe knew that the old man was a little drunk, and while he was a good client they knew that if he became too drunk he would leave without paying, so they kept watch on him.

"Last week he tried to commit suicide," one waiter said.

"Why?"

"He was in despair."

"What about?"

"Nothing."

"How do you know it was nothing?"

"He has plenty of money."

They sat together at a table that was close against the wall near the door of the cafe and looked at the terrace where the tables were all empty except where the old man sat in the shadow of the leaves of the tree that moved slightly in the wind. A girl and a soldier went by in the street. The street light shone on the brass number on his collar. The girl wore no head covering and hurried beside him.

"The guard will pick him up," one waiter said.

"What does it matter if he gets what he's after?"

"He had better get off the street now. The guard will get him. They went by five minutes ago."

The old man sitting in the shadow rapped on his saucer with his glass. The younger waiter went over to him.

"What do you want?"

The old man looked at him. "Another brandy," he said.

"You'll be drunk," the waiter said. The old man looked at him. The waiter went away.

"He'll stay all night," he said to his colleague. "I'm sleepy now. I never get into bed before three o'clock. He should have killed himself last week."

The waiter took the brandy bottle and another saucer from the counter inside the cafe and marched out to the old man's table. He put down the saucer and poured the glass full of brandy.

"You should have killed yourself last week," he said to the deaf man. The old man motioned with his finger. "A little more," he said. The waiter poured on into the glass so that the brandy slopped over and ran down the stem into the top saucer of the pile. "Thank you," the old man said. The waiter took the bottle back inside the cafe. He sat down at the table with his colleague again.

"He's drunk now," he said.

"He's drunk every night."

"What did he want to kill himself for?"

"How should I know."

"How did he do it?"

"He hung himself with a rope."

"Who cut him down?"

"His niece."

"Why did he do it?"

"For his soul."

"How much money has he got?"

"He's got plenty."

"He must be eighty years old."

"Anyway I should say he was eighty."

"I wish he would go home. I never get to bed before three o'clock. What kind of hour is that to go to bed?"

"He stays up because he likes it."

"He's lonely. I'm not lonely. I have a wife waiting in bed for me."

"He had a wife once too."

"A wife would be no good to him now."

"You can't tell. He might be better with a wife."

"His niece looks after him."

"I know. You said she cut him down."

"I wouldn't want to be that old. An old man is a nasty thing."

"Not always. This old man is clean. He drinks without spilling. Even now, drunk. Look at him."

"I don't want to look at him. I wish he would go home. He has no regard for those who must work."

The old man looked from his glass across the square, then over at the waiters.

"Another brandy," he said, pointing to his glass. The waiter who was in a hurry came over.

"Finished," he said, speaking with that omission of syntax stupid people employ when talking to drunken people or foreigners. "No more tonight. Close now."

"Another," said the old man.

"No. Finished." The waiter wiped the edge of the table with a towel and shook his head.

The old man stood up, slowly counted the saucers, took a leather coin purse from his pocket and paid for the drinks, leaving half a peseta tip.

The waiter watched him go down the street, a very old man walking unsteadily but with dignity.

"Why didn't you let him stay and drink?" the unhurried waiter asked. They were putting up the shutters. "It is not half-past two."

"I want to go home to bed."

"What is an hour?"

"More to me than to him."

"An hour is the same."

"You talk like an old man yourself. He can buy a bottle and drink at home."

"It's not the same."

"No, it is not," agreed the waiter with a wife. He did not wish to be unjust. He was only in a hurry.

"And you? You have no fear of going home before your usual hour?"

"Are you trying to insult me?"

"No, hombre, only to make a joke."

"No," the waiter who was in a hurry said, rising from putting on the metal shutters. "I have confidence. I am all confidence."

"You have youth, confidence, and a job," the older waiter said. "You have everything."

"And what do you lack?"

"Everything but work."

"You have everything I have."

"No. I have never had confidence and I'm not young."

"Come on. Stop talking nonsense and lock up."

"I am of those who like to stay late at the cafe," the older waiter said.

"With all those who do not want to go to bed. With all those who need a light for the night."

"I want to go home and into bed."

"We are of two different kinds," the older waiter said. He was now dressed to go home. "It is not only a question of youth and confidence although those things are very beautiful. Each night I am reluctant to close up because there may be someone who needs the cafe."

"Hombre, there are bodegas open all night long."

"You do not understand. This is a clean and pleasant cafe. It is well lighted. The light is very good and also, now, there are shadows of the leaves."

"Good night," said the younger waiter.

"Good night," the other said. Turning off the electric light he continued the conversation with himself.

It is the light of course but it is necessary that the place be clean and pleasant. You do not want music. Certainly you do not want music. Nor can you stand before a bar with dignity although that is all that is provided for these hours. What did he fear? It was not fear or dread. It was a nothing that he knew too well. It was all a nothing and a man was nothing too. It was only that and light was all it needed and a certain cleanness and order. Some lived in it and never felt it but he knew it all was nada y pues nada y nada y pues nada. Our nada who art in nada, nada be thy name thy kingdom nada thy will be nada in nada as it is in nada. Give us this nada our daily nada and nada us our nada as we nada our nadas and nada us not into nada but deliver us from nada; pues nada. Hail nothing full of nothing, nothing is with thee. He smiled and stood before a bar with a shining steam pressure coffee machine.

"What's yours?" asked the barman.

"Nada."

"Otro loco mass," said the barman and turned away.

"A little cup," said the waiter.

The barman poured it for him.

"The light is very bright and pleasant but the bar is unpolished," the waiter said.

The barman looked at him but did not answer. It was too late at night for conversation.

"You want another copita?" the barman asked.

"No, thank you," said the waiter and went out. He disliked bars and bodegas. A clean, well-lighted cafe was a very different thing. Now, without thinking further, he would go home to his room. He would lie in the bed and finally, with daylight, he would go to sleep. After all, he said to himself, it is probably only insomnia. Many must have it.

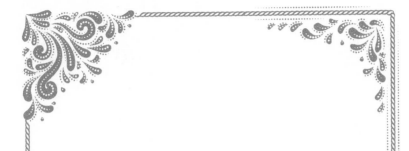

A DAY'S WAIT

He came into the room to shut the windows while we were still in bed and I saw he looked ill. He was shivering, his face was white, and he walked slowly as though it ached to move.

'What's the matter, Schatz?'

'I've got a headache.'

'You better go back to bed.' 'No, I'm all right.'

'You go to bed. I'll see you when I'm dressed.'

But when I came downstairs he was dressed, sitting by the fire, looking a very sick and miserable boy of nine years. When I put my hand on his forehead I knew he had a fever.

'You go up to bed,' I said, 'you're sick.'

'I'm all right,' he said.

When the doctor came he took the boy's temperature.

'What is it?' I asked him.

'One hundred and two.'

Downstairs, the doctor left three different medicines in different colored capsules with instructions for giving them. One was to bring down the fever, another a purgative, the third to overcome an acid condition. The germs of influenza can only exist in an acid condition, he explained. He seemed to know all about influenza and said there was nothing to worry about if the fever did not go above one hundred and four degrees. This was a light epidemic of flu and there was no danger if you avoided pneumonia.

Back in the room I wrote the boy's temperature down and made a note of the time to give the various capsules.

'Do you want me to read to you?'

'All right. If you want to,' said the boy. His face was very white and there were dark areas under his eyes. He lay still in bed and seemed very detached from what was going on.

I read aloud from Howard Pyle's *Book of Pirates;* but I could see he was not following what I was reading.

'How do you feel, Schatz?' I asked him.

'Just the same, so far,' he said.

I sat at the foot of the bed and read to myself while I waited for it to be time to give another capsule. It would have been natural for him to go to sleep, but when I looked up he was looking at the foot of the bed, looking very strangely.

'Why don't you try to go to sleep? I'll wake you up for the medicine.'

'I'd rather stay awake.'

After a while he said to me, 'You don't have to stay here with me, Papa, if it bothers you.'

'It doesn't bother me.'

'No, I mean you don't have to stay if it's going to bother you.'

I thought perhaps he was a little light-headed and after giving him the prescribed capsule at eleven o'clock I went out for a while. It was a bright, cold day, the ground covered with a sleet that had frozen so that it seemed as if all the bare trees, the bushes, the cut brush and all the grass and the bare ground had been varnished with ice. I took the young Irish setter for a little walk up the road and along a frozen creek, but it was difficult to stand or walk on the glassy surface and the red dog slipped and slithered and fell twice, hard, once dropping my gun and having it slide over the ice.

We flushed a covey of quail under a high clay bank with overhanging brush and killed two as they went out of sight over the top of the bank. Some of the covey lit the trees, but most of them scattered into brush piles and it was necessary to jump on the ice-coated mounds of brush several times before they would flush. Coming out while you were poised unsteadily on the icy, springy brush they made difficult shooting and killed two, missed five, and started back pleased to have found a covey close to the house and happy there were so many left to find on another day.

At the house they said the boy had refused to let anyone come into the room.

'You can't come in,' he said. 'You mustn't get what I have.'

I went up to him and found him in exactly the position I had left him, white-faced, but with the tops of his cheeks flushed by the fever, staring still, as he had stared, at the foot of the bed.

I took his temperature.

'What is it?'

'Something like a hundred,' I said. It was one hundred and two and four tenth.

'It was a hundred and two,' he said.

'Who said so?'

'The doctor.'

'Your temperature is all right,' I said. 'It's nothing to worry about.'

'I don't worry,' he said, 'but I can't keep from thinking.'

'Don't think,' I said. 'Just take it easy.'

'I'm taking it easy,' he said and looked straight ahead. He was evidently holding tight onto himself about something.

'Take this with water.'

'Do you think it will do any good?'

'Of course it will.'

I sat down and opened the Pirate book and commenced to read, but I could see he was not following, so I stopped.

'About what time do you think I'm going to die?' he asked.

'What?'

'About how long will it be before I die?'

'You aren't going to die. What's the matter with you?'

Oh, yes, I am. I heard him say a hundred and two.'

'People don't die with a fever of one hundred and two. That's a silly way to talk.'

'I know they do. At school in France the boys told me you can't live with forty-four degrees. I've got a hundred and two.'

He had been waiting to die all day, ever since nine o'clock in the morning.

'You poor Schatz,' I said. 'Poor old Schatz. It's like miles and kilometers. You aren't going to die. That's a different thermometer. On that thermometer thirty-seven is normal. On this kind it's ninety-eight.'

'Are you sure?'

'Absolutely,' I said. 'It's like miles and kilometers. You know, like how many kilometers we make when we do seventy in the car?'

'Oh,' he said.

But his gaze at the foot of his bed relaxed slowly. The hold over himself relaxed too, finally, and the next day it was very slack and he cried very easily at little things that were of no importance.

THE KILLERS

The door of Henry's lunchroom opened and two men came in. They sat down at the counter.

"What's yours?" George asked them.

"I don't know," one of the men said. "What do you want to eat, Al?"

"I don't know," said Al. "I don't know what I want to eat."

Outside it was getting dark. The streetlight came on outside the window. The two men at the counter read the menu. From the other end of the counter Nick Adams watched them. He had been talking to George when they came in.

"I'll have a roast pork tenderloin with apple sauce and mashed potatoes," the first man said.

"It isn't ready yet."

"What the hell do you put it on the card for?"

"That's the dinner," George explained. "You can get that at six o'clock."

George looked at the clock on the wall behind the counter.

"It's five o'clock."

"The clock says twenty minutes past five," the second man said.

"It's twenty minutes fast."

"Oh, to hell with the clock," the first man said. "What have you got to eat?"

"I can give you any kind of sandwiches," George said. "You can have ham and eggs, bacon and eggs, liver and bacon, or a steak."

"Give me chicken croquettes with green peas and cream sauce and mashed potatoes."

"That's the dinner."

"Everything we want's the dinner, eh? That's the way you work it."

"I can give you ham and eggs, bacon and eggs, liver—"

"I'll take ham and eggs," the man called Al said. He wore a derby hat and a black overcoat buttoned across the chest. His face was small and white and he had tight lips. He wore a silk muffler and gloves.

"Give me bacon and eggs," said the other man. He was about the same size as Al. Their faces were different, but they were dressed like twins. Both wore overcoats too tight for them. They sat leaning forward, their elbows on the counter.

"Got anything to drink?" Al asked.

"Silver beer, bevo, ginger-ale," George said.

"I mean you got anything to drink?"

"Just those I said."

"This is a hot town," said the other. "What do they call it?"

"Summit."

"Ever hear of it?" Al asked his friend.

"No," said the friend.

"What do they do here nights?" Al asked.

"They eat the dinner," his friend said. "They all come here and eat the big dinner."

"That's right," George said.

"So you think that's right?" Al asked George.

"Sure."

"You're a pretty bright boy, aren't you?"

"Sure," said George.

"Well, you're not," said the other little man. "Is he, Al?"

"He's dumb," said Al. He turned to Nick. "What's your name?"

"Adams."

49

"Another bright boy," Al said. "Ain't he a bright boy, Max?"

"The town's full of bright boys," Max said.

George put the two platters, one of ham and eggs, the other of bacon and eggs, on the counter. He set down two side dishes of fried potatoes and closed the wicket into the kitchen.

"Which is yours?" he asked Al.

"Don't you remember?"

"Ham and eggs."

"Just a bright boy," Max said. He leaned forward and took the ham and eggs. Both men ate with their gloves on. George watched them eat.

"What are you looking at?" Max looked at George.

"Nothing."

"The hell you were. You were looking at me."

"Maybe the boy meant it for a joke, Max," Al said.

George laughed.

"You don't have to laugh," Max said to him. "You don't have to laugh at all, see?"

"All right," said George.

"So he thinks it's all right." Max turned to Al. "He thinks it's all right. That's a good one."

"Oh, he's a thinker," Al said. They went on eating.

"What's the bright boy's name down the counter?" Al asked Max.

"Hey, bright boy," Max said to Nick. "You go around on the other side of the counter with your boy friend."

"What's the idea?" Nick asked.

"There isn't any idea."

"You better go around, bright boy," Al said. Nick went around behind the counter.

"What's the idea?" George asked.

"None of your damned business," Al said. "Who's out in the kitchen?"

"The nigger."

"What do you mean the nigger?"

"The nigger that cooks."

"Tell him to come in."

"What's the idea?"

"Tell him to come in."

"Where do you think you are?"

"We know damn well where we are," the man called Max said. "Do we look silly?"

"You talk silly," Al said to him. "What the hell do you argue with this kid for? Listen," he said to George, "tell the nigger to come out here."

"What are you going to do to him?"

"Nothing. Use your head, bright boy. What would we do to a nigger?"

George opened the slit that Opened back into the kitchen. "Sam," he called. "Come in here a minute."

The door to the kitchen opened and the nigger came in. "What was it?" he asked. The two men at the counter took a look at him.

"All right, nigger. You stand right there," Al said.

Sam, the nigger, standing in his apron, looked at the two men sitting at the counter. "Yes, sir," he said. Al got down from his stool.

"I'm going back to the kitchen with the nigger and bright boy," he said. "Go on back to the kitchen, nigger. You go with him, bright boy." The little man walked after Nick and Sam, the cook, back into the kitchen. The door shut after them. The man called Max sat at the counter opposite George. He didn't look at George but looked in the mirror that ran along back of the counter. Henry's had been made over from a saloon into a lunch counter.

"Well, bright boy," Max said, looking into the mirror, "why don't you say something?"

"What's it all about?"

"Hey, Al," Max called, "bright boy wants to know what it's all about."

"Why don't you tell him?" Al's voice came from the kitchen.

"What do you think it's all about?"

"I don't know."

"What do you think?"

Max looked into the mirror all the time he was talking.

"I wouldn't say."

"Hey, Al, bright boy says he wouldn't say what he thinks it's all about."

"I can hear you, all right," Al said from the kitchen. He had propped open the slit that dishes passed through into the kitchen with a catsup bottle. "Listen, bright boy," he said from the kitchen to George. "Stand a little further along the bar. You move a little to the left, Max." He was like a photographer arranging for a group picture.

"Talk to me, bright boy," Max said. "What do you think's going to happen?"

George did not say anything.

"I'll tell you," Max said. "We're going to kill a Swede. Do you know a big Swede named Ole Anderson?"

"Yes."

"He comes here to eat every night, don't he?"

"Sometimes he comes here."

"He comes here at six o'clock, don't he?"

"If he comes."

"We know all that, bright boy," Max said. "Talk about something else. Ever go to the movies?"

"Once in a while."

"You ought to go to the movies more. The movies are fine for a bright boy like you."

"What are you going to kill Ole Anderson for? What did he ever do to you?"

"He never had a chance to do anything to us. He never even seen us."

"And he's only going to see us once," Al said from the kitchen.

"What are you going to kill him for, then?" George asked.

"We're killing him for a friend. Just to oblige a friend, bright boy."

"Shut up," said Al from the kitchen. "You talk too goddamn much."

"Well, I got to keep bright boy amused. Don't I, bright boy?"

"You talk too damn much," Al said. "The nigger and my bright boy are amused by themselves. I got them tied up like a couple of girl friends in the convent."

"I suppose you were in a convent."

"You never know."

"You were in a kosher convent. That's where you were."

George looked up at the clock.

"If anybody comes in you tell them the cook is off, and if they keep after it, you tell them you'll go back and cook yourself. Do you get that, bright boy?"

"All right," George said. "What you going to do with us afterward?"

"That'll depend," Max said. "That's one of those things you never know at the time."

George looked up at the dock. It was a quarter past six. The door from the street opened. A streetcar motorman came in.

"Hello, George," he said. "Can I get supper?"

"Sam's gone out," George said. "He'll be back in about half an hour."

"I'd better go up the street," the motorman said. George looked at the clock. It was twenty minutes, past six.

"That was nice, bright boy," Max said. "You're a regular little gentleman."

"He knew I'd blow his head off," Al said from the kitchen.

"No," said Max. "It ain't that. Bright boy is nice. He's a nice boy. I like him."

At six-fifty-five George said: "He's not coming."

Two other people had been in the lunchroom. Once George had gone out to the kitchen and made a ham-and-egg sandwich "to go" that a man wanted to take with him. Inside the kitchen he saw Al, his derby hat tipped back, sitting on a stool beside the wicket with the muzzle of a sawed-off shotgun resting on the ledge. Nick and the cook were back to back in the corner, a towel tied in each of their mouths. George had cooked the sandwich, wrapped it up in oiled paper, put it in a bag, brought it in, and the man had paid for it and gone out.

"Bright boy can do everything," Max said. "He can cook and everything. You'd make some girl a nice wife, bright boy."

"Yes?" George said, "Your friend, Ole Anderson, isn't going to come."

"We'll give him ten minutes," Max said.

Max watched the mirror and the clock. The hands of the clock marked seven o'clock, and then five minutes past seven.

"Come on, Al," said Max. "We better go. He's not coming."

"Better give him five minutes," Al said from the kitchen.

In the five minutes a man came in, and George explained that the cook was sick.

"Why the hell don't you get another cook?" the man asked. "Aren't you running a lunch-counter?" He went out.

"Come on, Al," Max said.

"What about the two bright boys and the nigger?"

"They're all right."

"You think so?"

"Sure. We're through with it."

"I don't like it," said Al. "It's sloppy. You talk too much."

"Oh, what the hell," said Max. "We got to keep amused, haven't we?"

"You talk too much, all the same," Al said. He came out from the kitchen. The cut-off barrels of the shotgun made a slight bulge under the waist of his too tight-fitting overcoat. He straightened his coat with his gloved hands.

"So long, bright boy," he said to George. "You got a lot of luck."

"That's the truth," Max said. "You ought to play the races, bright boy."

The two of them went out the door. George watched them, through the window, pass under the arc- light and across the street. In their tight overcoats and derby hats they looked like a vaudeville team. George went back through the swinging door into the kitchen and untied Nick and the cook.

"I don't want any more of that," said Sam, the cook. "I don't want any more of that."

Nick stood up. He had never had a towel in his mouth before.

"Say," he said. "What the hell?" He was trying to swagger it off.

"They were going to kill Ole Anderson," George said. "They were going to shoot him when he came in to eat."

"Ole Anderson?"

"Sure."

The cook felt the corners of his mouth with his thumbs.

"They all gone?" he asked.

"Yeah," said George. "They're gone now."

"I don't like it," said the cook. "I don't like any of it at all"

"Listen," George said to Nick. "You better go see Ole Anderson."

"All right."

"You better not have anything to do with it at all," Sam, the cook, said. "You better stay way out of it."

"Don't go if you don't want to," George said.

"Mixing up in this ain't going to get you anywhere," the cook said. "You stay out of it."

"I'll go see him," Nick said to George. "Where does he live?"

The cook turned away.

"Little boys always know what they want to do," he said.

"He lives up at Hirsch's rooming-house," George said to Nick.

"I'll go up there."

Outside the arc-light shone through the bare branches of a tree. Nick walked up the street beside the car-tracks and turned at the next arc-light down a side-street. Three houses up the street was Hirsch's rooming-house. Nick walked up the two steps and pushed the bell. A woman came to the door.

"Is Ole Anderson here?"

"Do you want to see him?"

"Yes, if he's in."

Nick followed the woman up a flight of stairs and back to the end of a corridor. She knocked on the door.

"Who is it?"

"It's somebody to see you, Mr. Anderson," the woman said.

"It's Nick Adams."

"Come in."

Nick opened the door and went into the room. Ole Anderson was lying on the bed with all his clothes on. He had been a heavyweight prizefighter and he was too long for the bed. He lay with his head on two pillows. He did not look at Nick.

"What was it?" he asked.

"I was up at Henry's," Nick said, "and two fellows came in and tied up me and the cook, and they said they were going to kill you."

It sounded silly when he said it. Ole Anderson said nothing.

"They put us out in the kitchen," Nick went on. "They were going to shoot you when you came in to supper."

Ole Anderson looked at the wall and did not say anything.

"George thought I better come and tell you about it."

"There isn't anything I can do about it," Ole Anderson said.

"I'll tell you what they were like."

"I don't want to know what they were like," Ole Anderson said. He looked at the wall. "Thanks for coming to tell me about it."

"That's all right."

Nick looked at the big man lying on the bed.

"Don't you want me to go and see the police?"

"No," Ole Anderson said. "That wouldn't do any good."

"Isn't there something I could do?"

"No. There ain't anything to do."

"Maybe it was just a bluff."

"No. It ain't just a bluff."

Ole Anderson rolled over toward the wall.

"The only thing is," he said, talking toward the wall, "I just can't make up my mind to go out. I been here all day."

"Couldn't you get out of town?"

"No," Ole Anderson said. "I'm through with all that running around."

He looked at the wall.

"There ain't anything to do now."

"Couldn't you fix it up some way?"

"No. I got in wrong." He talked in the same flat voice. "There ain't anything to do. After a while I'll make up my mind to go out."

"I better go back and see George," Nick said.

"So long," said Ole Anderson. He did not look toward Nick. "Thanks for coming around."

Nick went out. As he shut the door he saw Ole Anderson with all his clothes on, lying on the bed looking at the wall.

"He's been in his room all day," the landlady said downstairs. "I guess he don't feel well. I said to him: 'Mr. Anderson, you ought to go out and take a walk on a nice fall day like this,' but he didn't feel like it."

"He doesn't want to go out."

"I'm sorry he don't feel well," the woman said. "He's an awfully nice man. He was in the ring, you know."

"I know it."

"You'd never know it except from the way his face is," the woman said.

They stood talking just inside the street door. "He's just as gentle."

"Well, good night, Mrs. Hirsch," Nick said.

"I'm not Mrs. Hirsch," the woman said. "She owns the place. I just look after it for her. I'm Mrs. Bell."

"Well, good night, Mrs. Bell," Nick said.

"Good night," the woman said.

Nick walked up the dark street to the corner under the arc-light, and then along the car-tracks to Henry's eating-house. George was inside, back of the counter.

"Did you see Ole?"

"Yes," said Nick. "He's in his room and he won't go out."

The cook opened the door from the kitchen when he heard Nick's voice.

"I don't even listen to it," he said and shut the door.

"Did you tell him about it?" George asked.

"Sure. I told him but he knows what it's all about."

"What's he going to do?"

"Nothing."

"They'll kill him."

"I guess they will."

"He must have got mixed up in something in Chicago."

"I guess so," said Nick.

"It's a hell of a thing!"

"It's an awful thing," Nick said.

They did not say anything. George reached down for a towel and wiped the counter.

"I wonder what he did?" Nick said.

"Double-crossed somebody. That's what they kill them for."

"I'm going to get out of this town," Nick said.

"Yes," said George. "That's a good thing to do."

"I can't stand to think about him waiting in the room and knowing he's going to get it. It's too damned awful."

"Well," said George, "you better not think about it."

INDIAN CAMP

At the lake shore there was another rowboat drawn up. The two Indians stood waiting.

Nick and his father got in the stern of the boat and the Indians shoved it off and one of them got in to row. Uncle George sat in the stern of the camp rowboat. The young Indian shoved the camp boat off and got in to row Uncle George.

The two boats started off in the dark. Nick heard the oarlocks of the other boat quite a way ahead of them in the mist. The Indians rowed with quick choppy strokes. Nick lay back with his father's arm around him. It was cold on the water. The Indian who was rowing them was working very hard, but the other boat moved further ahead in the mist all the time.

"Where are we going, Dad?" Nick asked.

"Over to the Indian camp. There is an Indian lady very sick."

"Oh," said Nick.

Across the bay they found the other boat beached. Uncle George was smoking a cigar in the dark. The young

Indian pulled the boat way up on the beach. Uncle George gave both the Indians cigars.

They walked up from the beach through a meadow that was soaking wet with dew, following the young Indian who carried a lantern. Then they went into the woods and followed a trail that led to the logging road that ran back into the hills. It was much lighter on the logging road as the timber was cut away on both sides. The young Indian stopped and blew out his lantern and they all walled on along the road.

They came around a bend and a dog came out barking. Ahead were the lights of the shanties where the Indian bark-peelers lived. More dogs rushed out at them. The two Indians sent them back to the shanties. In the shanty nearest the road there was a light in the window. An old woman stood in the doorway holding a lamp.

Inside on a wooden bunk lay a young Indian woman. She had been trying to have her baby for two days. All the old women in the camp had been helping her. The men had moved off up the road to sit in the dark and smoke cut of range of the noise she made. She screamed just as Nick and the two Indians followed his father and Uncle George into the shanty. She lay in the lower bunk, very big under a quilt. Her head was turned to one side. In the upper bunk was her husband. He had cut his foot very badly with an ax three days before. He was smoking a pipe. The room smelled very bad.

Nick's father ordered some water to be put on the stove, and while it was heating he spoke to Nick.

"This lady is going to have a baby, Nick," he said.

"I know," said Nick.

"You don't know," said his father. "Listen to me. What she is going through is called being in labor. The baby wants to be born and she wants it to be born. All her muscles are trying to get the baby born. That is what is happening when she screams."

"I see," Nick said.

Just then the woman cried out.

"Oh, Daddy, can't you give her something to make her stop screaming?" asked Nick.

"No. I haven't any anesthetic," his father said. "But her screams are not important. I don't hear them because they are not important."

The husband in the upper bunk rolled over against the wall.

The woman in the kitchen motioned to the doctor that the water was hot. Nick's father went into the kitchen and poured about half of the water out of the big kettle into a basin. Into the water left in the kettle he put several things he unwrapped from a handkerchief.

"Those must boil," he said, and began to scrub his hands in the basin of hot water with a cake of soap he had brought from the camp. Nick watched his father's hands scrubbing each other with the soap. While his father washed his hands very carefully and thoroughly, he talked.

"You see, Nick, babies are supposed to be born head first but sometimes they're not. When they're not they make a lot of trouble for everybody. Maybe I'll have to operate on this lady. We'll know in a little while."

When he was satisfied with his hands he went in and went to work.

"Pull back that quilt, will you, George?" he said. "I'd rather not touch it."

Later when he started to operate Uncle George and three Indian men held the woman still. She bit Uncle George on the arm and Uncle George said, "Damn squaw bitch!" and the young Indian who had rowed Uncle George over laughed at him. Nick held the basin for his father. It all took a long time.

His father picked the baby up and slapped it to make it breathe and handed it to the old woman.

"See, it's a boy, Nick," he said. "How do you like being an intern?"

Nick said. "All right." He was looking away so as not to see what his father was doing.

"There. That gets it," said his father and put something into the basin.

Nick didn't look at it.

"Now," his father said, "there's some stitches to put in. You can watch this or not, Nick, just as you like. I'm going to sew up the incision I made."

Nick did not watch. His curiosity had been gone for a long time.

His father finished and stood up. Uncle George and the three Indian men stood up. Nick put the basin out in the kitchen.

Uncle George looked at his arm. The young Indian smiled reminiscently.

"I'll put some peroxide on that, George," the doctor said.

He bent over the Indian woman. She was quiet now and her eyes were closed. She looked very pale. She did not know what had become of the baby or anything.

"I'll be back in the morning." the doctor said, standing up.

"The nurse should be here from St. Ignace by noon and she'll bring everything we need."

He was feeling exalted and talkative as football players are in the dressing room after a game.

"That's one for the medical journal, George," he said. "Doing a Caesarian with a jack-knife and sewing it up with nine-foot, tapered gut leaders."

Uncle George was standing against the wall, looking at his arm.

"Oh, you're a great man, all right," he said.

"Ought to have a look at the proud father. They're usually the worst sufferers in these little affairs," the doctor said. "I must say he took it all pretty quietly."

He pulled back the blanket from the Indian's head. His hand came away wet. He mounted on the edge of the lower bunk with the lamp in one hand and looked in. The Indian lay with his face toward the wall. His throat had been cut from ear to ear. The blood had flowed down into a pool where his body sagged the bunk. His head rested on his left arm. The open razor lay, edge up, in the blankets.

"Take Nick out of the shanty, George," the doctor said.

There was no need of that. Nick, standing in the door of the kitchen, had a good view of the upper bunk when his father, the lamp in one hand, tipped the Indian's head back.

It was just beginning to be daylight when they walked along the logging road back toward the lake.

"I'm terribly sorry I brought you along, Nickie," said his father, all his post-operative exhilaration gone. "It was an awful mess to put you through."

"Do ladies always have such a hard time having babies?" Nick asked.

"No, that was very, very exceptional."

"Why did he kill himself, Daddy?"

"I don't know, Nick. He couldn't stand things, I guess."

"Do many men kill themselves, Daddy?"

"Not very many, Nick."

"Do many women?"

"Hardly ever."

"Don't they ever?"

"Oh, yes. They do sometimes."

"Daddy?"

"Yes."

"Where did Uncle George go?"

"He'll turn up all right."

"Is dying hard, Daddy?"

"No, I think it's pretty easy, Nick. It all depends."

They were seated in the boat. Nick in the stern, his father rowing. The sun was coming up over the hills. A bass jumped, making a circle in the water. Nick trailed his hand in the water. It felt warm in the sharp chill of the morning.

In the early morning on the lake sitting in the stern of the boat with his father rowing; he felt quite sure that he would never die.

THE MOTHER
OF A QUEEN

When his father died he was only a kid and his manager buried him perpetually. That is, so he would have the plot permanently. But when his mother died his manager thought they might not always be so hot on each other. They were sweethearts; sure he's a queen, didn't you know that, of course he is. So he just buried her for five years.

Well, when he came back to Mexico from Spain he got the first notice. It said it was the first notice that the five years were up and would he make arrangements for the continuing of his mother's grave. It was only twenty dollars for perpetual. I had the cash box then and I said let me attend to it, Paco. But he said no, he would look after it. He'd look after it right away. It was his mother and he wanted to do it himself.

Then in a week he got the second notice. I read it to him and I said I thought he had looked after it.

No, he said, he hadn't.

"Let me do it," I said. "It's right here in the cash box."

No, he said. Nobody could tell him what to do. He'd do it himself when he got around to it. "What's the sense in spending money sooner than necessary?"

"All right," I said, "but see you look after it." At this time he had a contract for six fights at four thousand pesos a fight besides his benefit fight. He made over fifteen thousand dollars there in the capital alone. He was just tight, that's all.

The third notice came in another week and I read it to him. It said that if he did not make the payment by the following Saturday his mother's grave would be opened and her remains dumped on the common boneheap. He said he would go attend to it that afternoon when he went to town.

"Why not have me do it?" I asked him.

"Keep out of my business," he said. "It's my business and I'm going to do it."

"All right, if that's the way you feel about it," I said. "Do your own business."

He got the money out of the cash box, although then he always carried a hundred or more pesos with him all the time, and he said he would look after it. He went out with the money and so of course I thought he had attended to it.

A week later the notice came that they had no response to the final warning and so his mother's body had been dumped on the boneheap; on the public boneheap.

"Jesus Christ," I said to him, "you said you'd pay that and you took money out of the cash box to do it and now what's happened to your mother? My God, think of it! The public boneheap and your own mother. Why didn't you let me look after it? I would have sent it when the first notice came."

"It's none of your business. It's *my* mother."

"It's none of *my* business, yes, but it was *your* business. What kind of blood is it in a man that will let that be done to his mother? You don't deserve to have a mother."

"It is my mother," he said. "Now she is so much dearer to me. Now I don't have to think of her buried in one place and be sad. Now she is all about me in the air, like the birds and the flowers. Now she will always be with me."

"Jesus Christ," I said, "what kind of blood have you anyway? I don't want you to even speak to me."

"She is all around me," he said. "Now I will never be sad."

At that time he was spending all kinds of money around women trying to make himself seem a man and fool people, but it didn't have any effect on people that knew anything about him. He owed me over six hundred pesos and he wouldn't pay me. "Why do you want it now?" he'd say. "Don't you trust me? Aren't we friends?"

"It isn't friends or trusting you. It's that I paid the accounts out of my own money while you were away and now I need the money back and you have it to pay me."

"I haven't got it."

"You have it," I said. "It's in the cash box now and you can pay me."

"I need that money for something," he said. "You don't know all the needs I have for money."

"I stayed here all the time you were in Spain and you authorized me to pay these things as they came up, all these things of the house, and you didn't send any money while you were gone and I paid over six hundred pesos in my own money and now I need it and you can pay me."

"I'll pay you soon," he said. "Right now I need the money badly."

"For what?"

"For my own business."

"Why don't you pay me some on account?"

"I can't," he said. "I need that money too badly. But I will pay you."

He had only fought twice in Spain, they couldn't stand him there, they saw through him quick enough, and he had seven new fighting suits made and this is the kind of thing he was: he had them packed so badly that four of them were ruined by sea water on the trip back and he couldn't even wear them.

"My God," I said to him, "you go to Spain. You stay there the whole season and only fight two times. You spend all the money you took with you on suits and then have them spoiled by salt water so you can't wear them. That is the kind of season you have and then you talk to me about running your own business. Why don't you pay me the money you owe me so I can leave?"

"I want you here," he said, "and I will pay you. But now I need the money."

"You need it too badly to pay for your own mother's grave to keep your mother buried. Don't you?" I said.

"I am happy about what has happened to my mother," he said. "You cannot understand."

"Thank Christ I can't," I said. "You pay me what you owe me or I will take it out of the cash box."

"I will keep the cash box myself," he said.

"No, you won't," I said.

That very afternoon he came to me with a punk, some fellow from his own town who was broke, and said, "Here is a paesano who needs money to go home because his mother is very sick." This fellow was just a punk, you understand, a nobody he'd never seen before, but from his home town, and he wanted to be the big, generous matador with a fellow townsman.

"Give him fifty pesos from the cash box," he told me.

"You just told me you had no money to pay me," I said. "And now you want to give fifty pesos to this punk."

"He is a fellow townsman," he said, "and he is in distress."

"You bitch," I said. I gave him the key of the cash box. "Get it yourself. I'm going to town."

"Don't be angry," he said. "I'm going to pay you."

I got the car out to go to town. It was his car but he knew I drove it better than he did. Everything he did I could do better. He knew it. He couldn't even read and write. I was going to see somebody and see what I could do about making him pay me. He came out and said, "I'm coming with you and I'm going to pay you. We are good friends. There is no need to quarrel."

We drove into the city and I was driving. Just before we came into the town he pulled out twenty pesos.

"Here's the money," he said.

"You motherless bitch," I said to him and told him what he could do with the money. "You give fifty pesos to that punk and then offer me twenty when you owe me six hundred. I wouldn't take a nickel from you. You know what you can do with it."

I got out of the car without a peso in my pocket and I didn't know where I was going to sleep that night. Later I went out with a friend and got my things from his place. I never spoke to him again until this year. I met him walking with three friends in the evening on the way to the Callao cinema in the Gran Via in Madrid. He put his hand out to me.

"Hello Roger, old friend," he said to me. "How are you? People say you are talking against me. That you say all sorts of unjust things about me."

"All I say is you never had a mother," I said to him. That's the worst thing you can say to insult a man in Spanish.

"That's true," he said. "My poor mother died when I was so young it seems as though I never had a mother. It's very sad."

There's a queen for you. You can't touch them. Nothing, nothing can touch them. They spend money on themselves or for vanity, but they never pay. Try to get one to pay. I told him what I thought of him right there on the Gran Via, in front of three friends, but he speaks to me now when I meet him as though we were friends. What kind of blood is it that makes a man like that?

OTHER HARDBACK BOOKS

- Abraham Lincoln by Lord Charnwood
  Biographies/Leaders, ISBN: 9789387669147

- Alice's Adventures in Wonderland by Lewis Carroll
  Children's/Classics, ISBN: 9789387669055

- Awakened Imagination by Neville Goddard
  Religion & Spirituality, ISBN: 9789389157185

- Be What You Wish by Neville Goddard
  Mind, Body & Spirit, ISBN: 9789388118163

- Becoming a Writer by Dorothea Brande
  Self Help/General, ISBN: 9789389157192

- Believe in Yourself by Joseph Murphy
  Mind, Body & Spirit, ISBN: 9789388118439

- Black Beauty by Anna Sewell
  Children's/Classics, ISBN: 9789388118262

- Civilization and Its Discontents by Sigmund Freud
  Social Sciences/General, ISBN: 9789388118279

- Feeling is the Secret by Neville Goddard
  Religion & Spirituality, ISBN: 9789389157208

- Gravity by George Gamow
  Sciences/Physics, ISBN: 9789388118705

- Great Speeches of Abraham Lincoln by Abraham Lincoln
  History/United States, ISBN: 9789387669154

- How to Attract Money by Joseph Murphy
  Self Help/Success, ISBN: 9789388118446

- How to be Filled with the Holy Spirit by A.W. Tozer
  Religion/Christianity, ISBN: 9789389157215

- How to Develop Self-Confi. and Pub. Speaking by Dale Carnegie
  Mind, Body & Spirit, ISBN: 9789388118286

OTHER HARDBACK BOOKS

- How to Enjoy Your Life and Your Job by Dale Carnegie
  Self Help/General, ISBN: 9789388118293

- How to Stop Worrying and Start Living by Dale Carnegie
  Mind, Body & Spirit, ISBN: 9789387669161

- How to Win Friends and Influence People by Dale Carnegie
  Self Help/General, ISBN: 9789387669178

- Illust. Biography of William Shakespeare by Manju Gupta
  Biographies/Authors, ISBN: 9789387669246

- Madhubala by Manju Gupta
  Biographies/Cinems, ISBN: 9789387669253

- Meditations by Marcus Aurelius
  Non Fiction/Philosopy, ISBN: 9789388118781

- Mein Kampf by Adolf Hitler
  Autobiographies/Leaders, ISBN: 9789387669260

- My Experiments with Truth by Mahatma Gandhi
  Autobiographies/Leaders, ISBN: 9789387669277

- My Inventions: The Autobio. of Nikola Tesla by Nikola Tesla
  Autobiographies/Scientists, ISBN: 9789388118187

- Relativity by Albert Einstein
  Sciences/Physics, ISBN: 9789387669185

- Sense and Sensibility by Jane Austen
  Fiction/Classics, ISBN: 9789387669109

- The Alchemy of Happiness by Al-Ghazzali
  Religion & Spirituality, ISBN: 9789388118309

- The Art of Public Speaking by Dale Carnegie
  Self Help/General, ISBN: 9789388118477

- The Art of War by Sun Tzu
  Self Help/Success, ISBN: 9789387669321

OTHER HARDBACK BOOKS

- The Autobiography of a Yogi by Paramahansa Yogananda
  Autobiographies/General, ISBN: 9789387669192

- The Diary of a Young Girl by Anne Frank
  Autobiographies/Memoirs, ISBN: 9789387669208

- The Dynamic Laws of Prosperity by Catherine Ponder
  Mind, Body & Spirit, ISBN: 9789388118194

- The Elements of Style by William Strunk
  Non Fiction/Skill, ISBN: 9789389157222

- The Game of Life and How to Play It by Florence Scovel Shinn
  Mind, Body & Spirit, ISBN: 9789388118316

- The Imitation of Christ by Thomas À Kempis
  Religion/Christianity, ISBN: 9789388118200

- The Knowledge of the Holy by A.W. Tozer
  Religion/Christianity, ISBN: 9789389157239

- The Magic of Believing by Claudie Bristol
  Religion/Christianity, ISBN: 9789388118217

- The Magic of Faith by Joseph Murphy
  Mind, Body & Spirit, ISBN: 9789388118712

- The Miracles of Your Mind by Joseph Murphy
  Mind, Body & Spirit, ISBN: 9789387669215

- The Origin of Species by Charles Darwin
  Sciences/Life Sciences, ISBN: 9789387669345

- The Path of Prosperity by James Allen
  Mind, Body & Spirit, ISBN: 9789388118323

- The Power of Awareness by Neville Goddard
  Mind, Body & Spirit, ISBN: 9789388118330

- The Power of Concentration by Theron Q. Dumont
  Self Help/General, ISBN: 9789388118224

OTHER HARDBACK BOOKS

- The Power of Positive Thinking by Norman Vincent Peale
  Mind, Body & Spirit, ISBN: 9789388118729

- The Power of Your Subconscious Mind by Joseph Murphy
  Mind, Body & Spirit, ISBN: 9789387669222

- The Psychopathology of Everyday Life by Sigmund Freud
  Non Fiction/Psychology, ISBN: 9789388118231

- The Pursuit of God by A.W. Tozer
  Religion/Christianity, ISBN: 9789389157246

- The Quick and Easy Way to Effec. Speaking by Dale Carnegie
  Self Help/General, ISBN: 9789388118347

- The Richest Man in Babylon by George S. Clason
  Business & Economics, ISBN: 9789388118354

- The Science of Getting Rich by Wallace D. Wattles
  Self Help/Success, ISBN: 9789387669239

- The Seven Laws of Teaching by John Milton Gregory
  Self Help/General, ISBN: 9789388118460

- The Upanishads by Swami Paramananda
  Religion/Hinduism, ISBN: 9789388118774

- The World as I See It by Albert Einstein
  Non Fiction/Philosopy, ISBN: 9789388118248

- Think and Grow Rich by Napoleon Hill
  Self Help/Success, ISBN: 9789387669352

- Thought Vibration by William Walker Atkinson
  Non Fiction/Philosopy, ISBN: 9789389157253

- Wake Up and Live! by Dorothea Brande
  Mind, Body & Spirit, ISBN: 9789388118255

- Your Faith is Your Fortune by Neville Goddard
  Religion & Spirituality, ISBN: 9789389157260

CPSIA information can be obtained
at www.ICGtesting.com
Printed in the USA
LVHW111651301222
736207LV00002B/83